CAREFUL WHAT YOU WISH FOR

CAREFUL WHAT YOU WISH FOR

MAHTAB NARSIMHAN

ORCA **&**
ANCHOR

ORCA BOOK PUBLISHERS

Published in Canada and the United States
in 2022 by Orca Book Publishers.
orcabook.com

Library and Archives Canada Cataloguing in Publication
Title: Careful what you wish for / Mahtab Narsimhan.
Names: Narsimhan, Mahtab, author.
Description: Series statement: Orca anchor
Identifiers: Canadiana (print) 20210352795 | Canadiana (ebook)
20210352809 | ISBN 9781459834002 (softcover) |
ISBN 9781459834019 (PDF) | ISBN 9781459834026 (EPUB)
Classification: LCC PS8627.A77 C37 2022 | DDC jC813/.6—dc23

Library of Congress Control Number: 2021949084

Summary: In this high-interest accessible novel for teen readers,
a lonely teen stumbles onto a website that makes wishes come true.

Orca Book Publishers is committed to reducing the consumption
of nonrenewable resources in the production of our books. We make every
effort to use materials that support a sustainable future.

Orca Book Publishers gratefully acknowledges the support
for its publishing programs provided by the following agencies:
the Government of Canada, the Canada Council for the Arts and
the Province of British Columbia through the BC Arts Council
and the Book Publishing Tax Credit.

Edited by Tanya Trafford
Design by Ella Collier
Cover photography by Getty Images/gawrav
Author photo by Dean Macdonnell of Macdonnell Photography

Printed and bound in Canada.

25 24 23 22 • 1 2 3 4

For my squad:

Deborah, Frieda, Helaine and Karen

Chapter One

Eshana stared at the computer screen. The words in front of her made no sense. Her mind was back at school. Why hadn't she tied her shoelace? Of course Cara captured her face-plant in the lunchroom with her phone.

Eshana knew this wasn't over. Cara would use this to embarrass her.

"I *wish* I'd been more careful," said Eshana to herself. "I *wish* I could have today to do over."

Without realizing it, she'd typed the words *I wish* in the search bar. A link to a website called *I-WISH* was at the top of the list of hits. An animated wizard next to the link smiled. He looked harmless, but did she dare enter this website? It was a bad idea to join unknown websites. Anything could happen. The last thing she needed was for her computer to get hacked. Or destroyed by a virus.

Eshana closed the browser and went back to her math homework. She loved math. Numbers did not act weird. They behaved as they should. Not like people. Sometimes they said they were your friend. But acted like your enemy.

All the things that had gone wrong that day played over and over in her head. "I wish—" she started to say and then opened the browser again. This time she did not hesitate. She clicked on the link.

The website layout looked like fairyland. Eshana smiled. It reminded her of the books she used to read when she was much younger. She'd had enough of tenth grade and of jerks like Cara. She needed fun and simple. This was perfect.

A wishing well stood in the center of the home page. Words floated out of it, stayed on the screen for a few seconds, then vanished.

Welcome, one and all! This is a safe place. Look around, explore and make friends. Enjoy!

A castle nestled in a forest. The pathway was lit by fairy lights. Tree trunks had little doorways. In another corner was an inn called The Red Rabbit. A waterfall shimmered at the bottom right of the screen. As Eshana moved her cursor, messages appeared. *Knock Here, Enter Here* and, the best one, *Make a Wish.*

To the right of the screen there was a chat bar. She saw names like Black Kitten, Ghost Who Walks and Beetle King. One of them made her smile. It was her favorite afternoon snack, Tea & Toast. The avatar was a piece of toast.

It all seemed friendly and harmless. But her computer science teacher had warned her about websites designed to lure you in. This was probably the kind of thing she meant.

Her phone pinged. Eshana's best friend, Pia, had forwarded her a video clip. It was Eshana face-planting in slow motion.

Cara is sending this to everyone. What a loser. Let's start planning our revenge.

I hate her.

After replying, Eshana dropped the phone on her bed. Cara was the worst. And Eshana was her latest victim. *Everyone* would see the meme. Her life would suck even more.

A box popped up in the middle of the computer screen. It was asking her to fill in a name and upload a picture. Eshana typed in *Raven*, leaving the picture blank. It was Pia's name for her because of her black hair. Who knew what would happen next? Anything was better than thinking about her crappy day.

She started a private chat with Tea & Toast.

Hi, Tea & Toast. Cool name! I'm Raven.

Hey, Raven! Thanks. Call me T&T.

What's the deal here? Is it legit?

It's fun. But I don't hang out long.

Have you made any wishes yet? I have a gazillion.

Go slow. Look around first.

Eshana was feeling reckless. The fact that no one could see her felt awesome. She could be whomever she wanted.

Nah! Don't know slow. Who runs this chat room?

Before T&T could reply, a wizard avatar joined their chat.

Welcome to my website, Raven! If you have any wishes, you're in the right place!

Dude, private chat! Who're you?

Call me Wise One. I'm your guide within I-WISH. How can I help you?

Now things were getting interesting.

Chapter Two

Eshana did think it was rude that Wise One had just barged in. But she figured she'd better be polite if she didn't want to get kicked out.

Hello, Wise One. I like your site!

She was feeling bold. Her parents had warned her about safety online and in person. So had their teacher. But she was home and safe in her room. She could always log off if things got weird.

Thanks Raven. This is a safe space. Don't worry about anything. There is only one rule you must remember.

Rules already? Eshana thought.

?

Always speak the truth.

. Well that wasn't hard.

Was T&T seeing this exchange? Eshana could no longer see the toast avatar. Before Eshana could reach out to check, Wise One replied.

Why don't you tell me what you want, Raven? Start with something simple. That way I can quickly prove this site is not a fake.

I want my own squad.

I'm afraid I don't understand, Raven. Are you looking for police protection?

How old was this geezer?

FRIENDS! Lots of them.

Ah! Got it. Please type it out in the chat box. Try not to make spelling errors. You really don't want a squid following you around.

Wise *Ass* was more like it. Eshana's fingers flew over the keyboard. As soon as she stopped, gold stars burst from the wishing well. Her words disappeared.

After a few moments, another note from Wise One appeared.

Your wish has been granted. Now I must run. Someone's waiting for me at Waterfall Way. Come back soon, Raven. I think we're going to be good friends.

T&T reappeared in the chat. Eshana started typing.

Sweet or what? You get any wishes from Grandpa, T&T?

Um, yes, one. Just be careful, Raven.

Come on! Enchanted Forest, Fairy Grove and Waterfall Way? Feel like I've walked into a fairy tale!

There's a villain in every story.

You're avoiding my Q. What did *you* wish for?

Can't say. Been hearing things.

Then why still here?

T&T typed in a shrug emoji and logged off.

Hmm, thought Eshana. That was a bit weird. But then, so was her chat with Wise One. What had she stepped into? Was this a terrible idea? Should she delete her profile?

Eshana lay back on her bed and picked up her phone. As soon as the screen came to life, the face-plant meme played again. The terrible day came flooding back.

She would need more friends than just Pia to defeat the evil Queen Cara.

If only her wish would come true. How cool would that be?

Chapter Three

Math class was her favorite, and today they were doing algebra. She finished all the problems in half an hour.

"Yo!" someone whispered.

Eshana's heart almost stopped beating. Ryan was staring at her and tapping his paper. He normally hung out at the back of the class. But today he was sitting across the row from her. He looked so good in khakis and a white T-shirt. They showed off his deep brown skin.

What? she mouthed.

Help, he mouthed back, giving her a lopsided smile.

Eshana glanced at the math teacher. He was staring at his laptop, paying no attention to the class.

She slid her paper over to the edge of the desk and tilted it. Ryan stared at the paper and scribbled on his own sheet.

"Thanks!" he whispered. "You're the best!"

Eshana shrugged as if it was no big deal. But her insides were on fire. She imagined what it would be like to kiss him.

"You shouldn't have done that," said a quiet voice behind her.

Eshana glanced at the speaker. It was Tito. Eshana thought they were pretty cool. They had pink streaks in their hair and a nose ring. They were great with computers. They helped the teachers with software upgrades and stuff like that. But today Eshana just felt irritated with them.

"Mind your own business," she said, glaring.

The bell rang, and the teacher collected all their papers.

"Thanks for your help," said Ryan, catching up with Eshana outside. "If I'd effed up one more test, I'd have to take extra classes. Join me for lunch?"

There was a loud gasp behind her. Eshana turned around. Cara stood there with her friends, staring at Ryan.

Yes!

"You're inviting *her* to join you for lunch?" said Cara. "Are you serious? Have you checked your feed?"

What a cow! If he hadn't seen the video, he sure would now. *Die, Cara, DIE!*

"Mind your own business, Cara," said Ryan. "Coming, Eshana?"

"Sure," said Eshana, her heart pounding so hard she could barely hear what Ryan said. "Sure. I'll meet you there." She wanted to go to the washroom first to check her hair. Maybe put on a bit of gloss too.

"What's up, girl?"

It was a girl named Callie. She had never spoken to Eshana before.

"Same shit, different day," Eshana replied, trying to sound cool.

"You said it," said Callie.

On the way to the lunchroom, a couple more classmates waved and smiled. Eshana felt giddy. It must be her wish! *Thank you, old Wise One!* Today was already so much better than the day before.

Someone called out to her. It was Pia.

"Hey, what's up?" she asked. "Did you kill the Queen Bee? You look so happy."

"Ryan asked me to join him for lunch!"

Pia's shriek made a teacher passing by

give them a look. "Whaaaat? I want to know *everything* after school. Promise you won't hold out on me!"

Eshana promised and ran to the lunch-room. She made herself slow down as she joined Ryan at his table.

Lunch was amazing. She didn't remember what she ate or if she ate anything at all. Ryan told her about his life in Kenya before he'd moved here. It all sounded so cool.

"Now tell me about *your* time in India, Esh," said Ryan, leaning closer.

His voice sent a warm tingle down her spine. She didn't care that he'd shortened her name. He was interested in her life. In *her*.

As they sat there, students she'd never spoken to said hello or waved as they passed by. It was as if she was no longer invisible.

Cara shot Eshana a look. *Uh-oh.* Eshana knew Cara liked being at the top. She wouldn't like Eshana stealing the spotlight. She wondered what Cara would do as payback this time.

After school Eshana needed to get home and chat with Wise One. She slipped out the side door. She hoped she wouldn't run into Pia. She had another wish, and she couldn't wait to get online.

Chapter Four

Eshana started eating before her mom had even finished serving up dinner.

"What's the hurry?" her mom asked.

"Homework," said Eshana. Mom would never argue with that. It was a magic word she used often.

Dad wasn't home yet. He usually had to

work late. Eshana excused herself as soon as she was done.

She raced to her room and logged on to *I-WISH*. It was crowded today. Lots of people were in various areas of the site. She scrolled through the names and found Tea & Toast.

T&T! You were wrong!

Hey, Raven! What do you mean?

Had a great day!

Tell me.

Cute guy in class—Ryan. Totally into me. Also, I have friends. Note the plural. 😊😊😊

The cursor on their chat blinked. And blinked. And blinked.

Still there?

You're telling me you had no friends before?
I call BS.

Shit! Eshana had been meaning to text Pia and apologize. She wasn't really sorry. But Pia was her best friend. Eshana owed her an explanation.

Not the same as having a squad. More is good, right?

No free stuff here or anywhere, Raven. Not getting good vibes.

So leave.

I might just do that.

The wizard avatar popped into their private chat again. Eshana sucked in her breath. Grandpa was nosy! But it was his site, and she wanted her next wish.

What's this about vibes, T&T? I've tried hard to make this a fun place. If you're not having fun, you are free to leave.

T&T did not reply. Eshana didn't know what to say. It was weird how Wise One popped in and out of private chats. And his tone was not friendly this time.

Still waiting, T&T. I don't like being ignored.

I'm beat, Wise One. Bye, all.

T&T left the chat. Wise One continued on with Eshana.

Hope you had a good day, Raven. Was it everything you wished for?

Yes, it was dope!

I do not approve of drugs of any kind, Raven. Please tell me you aren't into that nonsense.

Relax, Wise One. I had a great day. My wish came true!

I would like to hear about it. When you are happy, my heart fills with joy.

He sounded like a Hallmark card. Cheesy. But Eshana still gave him all the details. Except for standing up Pia. He didn't need to know about broken promises.

Ready for your next wish?

Eshana knew exactly what she wanted, but something made her hesitate.

Let me look around a bit. BRB

Why can't kids learn how to speak in complete words and sentences?

Sheesh.

Be right back.

Knock on the yellow door of the Faraway Tree when you're ready for your next wish.

Eshana typed a thumbs-up emoji and then wandered through the site. Everywhere she looked, people were sharing their dreams and desires. Ghost Who Walks wanted a girl to fall in love with him. Black Kitten needed to ace an exam. Beetle King hoped for a baby brother.

This is harmless, thought Eshana. Here were ordinary people like her, sharing their wishes. No one laughed at them or judged them. T&T was full of shit, warning her about bad vibes.

Eshana happened to glance at the time at the bottom of her screen. *Crap!* She'd been on the site for an hour already. It had felt like only a minute. Where had the time gone? She texted Pia.

Forgot about our meeting. SORRY! Make it up to you tomorrow. xoxoxo

No response. Eshana wasn't worried. Pia was quick to forgive. But she was worried about Cara. No one showed up the queen and lived to tell the tale. Cara was ruthless. Eshana headed over to the Faraway Tree. A private chat popped up.

Hello, Raven.

I'm ready for my second wish, Wise One.

Type it out and be clear.

First, a question.

Yes?

What's in it for you?

When you're happy, I'm happy. Your feelings feed my soul.

Weird, thought Eshana. But things were looking up. Her next wish would make things even better.

I want Cara to stop making my life hell. She can disappear, for all I care.

A sparkle of silver stars wiped her words away.

Done, dear one! Enjoy tomorrow. It'll be even better than today.

Eshana checked her phone. No response from Pia. Maybe she *was* still mad. Just because Eshana stood her up one lousy time? Or was there another reason? Maybe Pia was jealous of Eshana's new friends. That made sense. The more she thought about it, the angrier Eshana felt. She punched her pillow. And then again. She felt a little better.

Just before she fell asleep, somewhere in the distance, she heard laughter.

Chapter Five

Eshana hurried to school the next day. Her stomach churned. Would Cara give her hell? Would Pia talk to her? Would Ryan invite her to join him for lunch again?

The corridors were full of students getting ready for class. A few high-fived Eshana. Queen Cara and her loyal subjects were nowhere around.

Eshana grabbed her books from her locker. When she slammed it shut, there was Tito. They looked serious. "You heard about Cara?"

Eshana's heart jumped into her throat. She hoped she didn't look too guilty. "No, er, has she left town?"

"Cara was in an accident last night," said Tito. "A bad one. Both legs broken. Might even have a head injury. She'll be gone for the rest of the year." Tito stared at Eshana in an odd way, almost as if they knew something.

Eshana's first reaction was joy. *No more Cara!* But as the news sank in, she felt cold. And afraid. Wise One had granted her wish, but she hadn't wanted *this*! She slumped against her locker, feeling light-headed.

"You okay?" said Tito. "If you're feeling faint, the nurse's station is more comfortable."

"I'm okay," she said. "Gotta run."

Eshana managed to get to the nearest bathroom before she threw up. She had wanted Cara gone, and it had come true. Was this a coincidence? She stared at herself in the mirror. Cara would have made some comment about Eshana's outfit. Now Eshana wouldn't have to worry about things like that. For a moment she felt bad for feeling happy about Cara's accident. But the feeling went away.

She made it to her class and sat down.

When Cara's two closest friends passed by her desk, they didn't giggle or snap pictures. They both had puffy eyes and weren't wearing any makeup.

"Hi, Eshana," said Ryan, sitting at his usual spot across from her. "You heard about Cara? Terrible, hey?"

Eshana wanted to say yes, but something inside her resisted. She felt an intense chill. "Nope. Cara was super mean to me and deserves what she got."

Ryan stared at her. Eshana looked away. Where had those awful words come from? She hadn't meant to say them.

Someone *else* was staring at her. Tito. They had a curious expression on their face.

Once again she got the feeling they knew more than they were saying. She hated how they made her feel.

"What?" snapped Eshana. Cara had been mean to Tito as well, making fun of their hair and jewelry. "What're you staring at?"

Tito shrugged. "There's no need to get angry."

"I'M NOT ANGRY!" Eshana hadn't meant to yell at Tito. Now everyone was looking at her. She grabbed her bag and took off again before she barfed in front of the class.

In the bathroom, Eshana stared at her white face. Why was she so angry now? What was happening to her? She heard distant laughter. Was that in her head or coming from someone in the hall? She peeked outside. No one was around. She shivered. Maybe she had the flu.

Somehow Eshana made it to lunchtime. She hurried to find Pia. Her friend would know what to do. In the lunchroom, Pia was surrounded by a bunch of tenth graders. They were talking about taking a ski trip on the weekend.

"Hey, Eshana, why don't you join us?" said Gina. "It'll be fun."

Eshana slipped into the seat beside Pia, who gave her a cool smile. So she was still mad at her. At least the others weren't.

"How much does it cost?" asked Eshana.

"Five hundred dollars," said Gina. "That's a cheap price for that place. Mom has connections. It includes everything."

Five hundred dollars. No way would Mom sign off on that kind of money for a ski trip. But Pia was going. Maybe if Eshana went too, she could patch things up.

"Can I let you know tomorrow?" said Eshana.

"Sure," said Gina.

Eshana knew what her next wish would be. Surely a few hundred dollars for a ski trip couldn't harm anyone.

Chapter Six

Eshana stared at her computer screen. Her second wish had come true. Cara was gone, although in a terrible way. Ryan seemed angry at her, and Pia was being a drama queen. Even though a lot of people were being nice to her, she missed her best friend.

Part of Eshana was worried her next wish would go wrong. But how could it? It was just money. Her head pounded. Maybe T&T could help. She logged on to *I-WISH*.

She noticed there were fewer people today. That was weird. And no sign of T&T. She looked all over the website. Just her luck—she really needed advice.

Hello, Raven!

Hey, Wise One.

Let me guess. You had the best day and would like to share it with a friend. I'm all ears.

It was okay. Have you seen T&T?

I had to ban them from this site for breaking the rules. But I hope you and I can be friends for a long time to come.

Another cheesy Hallmark response. He sounded creepy. T&T had warned her about this. But what if she asked for money for the ski trip as her last wish? She'd make it up to Pia and then *never* come back. Sounded like a good plan.

You're very quiet, Raven. Is everything all right?

I want to know how this wish thing works.

What do you mean? I give you something you want, and you give me something I want. We're both happy.

He was avoiding her question. Talking in riddles. Eshana tried once more.

I've been talking crap to my friends. It's as if someone is putting words in my mouth. I've even heard someone laughing in my head. It all started the day I logged on here.

The cursor blinked a few times. Eshana

wondered if he'd left the chat. But then more words appeared.

It's called speaking the truth, my dear! Most times we hide our thoughts and desires to be polite. I help people be themselves. Promise me you will keep coming back. We both need each other.

What the hell? This chat was getting more confusing by the minute. She wished T&T were around. She had so many questions.

I sense you have another wish, Raven. Write it down.

Fine. Here goes nothing, thought Eshana. She'd make one last wish and then never come back.

I want to be rich.

As before, sparkles appeared over her words and wiped them away.

Your wish is granted, Raven. When you're spending all that money, remember to thank me. Next time you log on, please bring a friend. The more, the merrier.

Eshana logged off and threw her laptop on the bed. It felt as if she had touched something dirty. In the washroom she scrubbed her hands—twice. Had she made a mistake asking for this last wish? Being rich would help the entire family, right?

Chapter Seven

The next day at school, Eshana kept waiting for something bad to happen. Nothing did. But as far as she knew, she wasn't rich either. Maybe it *was* all too good to be true.

But she still seemed to be popular. Ryan asked for her help in computer programming. Many students said hi to her in the hallways.

In class, Gina stopped by her desk. "So, you in?"

"Damn, I *knew* I'd forgotten something," Eshana lied. "Can I let you know tonight?" She had no idea how this wish would come true. Maybe her mom would call and tell her they'd discovered oil in their backyard.

"Okay," said Gina. "But Mom's making the booking this evening. Don't forget."

"Hey, it's not like you're booking the last flight to the moon," said Eshana. "Just give me some time, okay?"

Gina stared. Eshana felt her face grow hot. She'd done it again! She didn't even know she was *thinking* those words. "Kidding!" she said with a feeble laugh.

Gina just turned and walked away.

What was going on? Eshana had never felt so out of control. It had all started with *I-WISH*. Had the site really freed her to "tell the truth?" Or had it turned her into a Cara? Bitchy.

Eshana was afraid to open her mouth. If only Pia were talking to her. She'd have someone to help her figure this out.

Eshana headed to the last class of the day—computer science. She loved the teacher, Ms. Buckley. She made programming really fun. Eshana and Tito quickly solved every problem Ms. Buckley put up on the board. Eshana started thinking about wishes…

"Eshana, I asked you a question," said Ms. Buckley. "Are you paying attention?"

"You're boring me to death," Eshana replied. "So…no."

The class went silent.

"What did you say?"

Eshana felt every student's eyes on her. *Oh no.* Her mouth had a mind of its own. She tried to apologize. What came out instead was, "Stop asking silly questions and get on with the lesson."

Ms. Buckley turned white. Her eyes started to fill with tears. Eshana was close to tears herself. She glanced over at Tito, who shook their head. But there was something in their eyes. Something that told Eshana they understood exactly what was going on.

Just then there was a knock on the door. The principal's assistant stepped into the classroom. How did she know what had just happened? She spoke quietly to the teacher, and then they both looked at Eshana.

"The principal needs to see you right away," said Ms. Buckley. Her expression scared Eshana. This was not about her being rude. "Take all your things with you. We'll discuss your behavior some other time."

With a pounding heart, Eshana threw her books into her backpack. She was grateful for the interruption.

The assistant walked her to the office. Suddenly Eshana felt cold all over. What if this had something to do with her wish?

Eshana was surprised to see her mom's friend in the principal's office. "Why are you here, Dina Aunty?" asked Eshana. She felt faint.

Dina Aunty stood up right away. "Your father has had a heart attack. He's in the hospital. Your mother is with him. They asked me to bring you right away."

Eshana stumbled, but Dina Aunty caught her in time and hugged her close. "It's okay. I'm here for you."

Her father was fit and healthy. How could he have a heart attack? How bad was it? Was he going to die?

"I am so sorry," said the principal. "I can only imagine what a shock—"

"You can't imagine anything, so shut up!" said Eshana, pulling away from Dina Aunty.

The others stared at her. Eshana shivered. There was that chill inside her again. Every time she felt it, someone else seemed to control her thoughts and her words.

Chapter Eight

Her dad was in the intensive care unit. Her mom was sitting in the waiting room. She held her head in her hands.

"Eshana," she said, hugging her tight and sobbing. "Your father collapsed at work, and the supervisor called me. The doctors say we made it here just in time. We can only pray that the medicines and care work. I don't know what I would do if—"

"Stop crying," said Eshana, pulling away. "You're acting like some heroine in a Hindi movie."

Her mother froze. Eshana clamped her hands to her mouth. Mom was suffering, and instead of comforting her, she'd made her feel worse. She was a monster!

Her mom hurried away to the nearest washroom. Dina Aunty looked at her with disgust. "I don't know what has gotten into you, Eshana. First you are rude to the principal. And now to your mother. Just when she needs you the most! I realize this is a huge shock, so I'll let it go. But you will apologize to your mother when she gets back. If I ever hear you talk like that to her again, you will have me to deal with."

Eshana nodded. She kept her lips clamped shut. No way was she uttering a single word. She would only hurt the people she loved.

A doctor came into the waiting room, a tablet in his hand. "Mr. Suneesh Mehra is awake. Are you his family?"

When Eshana only nodded, Dina Aunty replied. "This is Suneesh's daughter, Eshana Mehra."

"You can go in for a minute," said the doctor. "But do not say *anything* to excite or upset him. He is very weak."

Eshana ran past the doctor. *Please let Dad be okay*, she repeated in her head. *And*

*please don't let me say anything that will
upset him.*

Her dad looked gray and exhausted. Wires
from his arm connected him to various
machines, which beeped and hummed. He
tried to smile, but the effort was too much.
He closed his eyes and breathed deeply. After
a few minutes, his eyes flickered open.

Eshana wanted to tell him he would be
okay, that she loved him. But she was afraid
of the words that might spill out. Instead
she laid her head on his chest gently. His
heart was still beating. Tears slid down her
face.

"Listen to me, Eshana," her dad said softly.
"If I don't make it..." He paused to catch his
breath. "There are papers. In my home office,

in the bottom drawer. You and Ma will be very comfortable. Look after her, okay?"

Eshana sat upright, her heart pounding. *Oh no.* He meant life insurance. So *this* was how her family was going to be rich. *She* had made this happen. All because of a lousy ski trip. If her father died, it would be all her fault.

She kissed her father's forehead and slipped out of the room. She still didn't dare speak. But what if this was the last time she saw him? She would regret not telling him she loved him.

I wish I had never found I-WISH.

When Eshana came out of the ICU, she saw her mom talking to Pia. As soon as Pia saw Eshana, she ran toward her and hugged her.

"I'm so sorry about your dad," said Pia. "I came as soon as I heard."

Eshana opened her mouth to say something but quickly closed it again. She dug into her backpack for a notebook and pen. Pia looked confused.

Eshana scribbled, *I am so sorry for being mean. I'm in big trouble. Help. Don't tell Mom or Dina Aunty.*

Pia nodded and hid the note as soon as the adults approached them.

"Mrs. Mehra, would it be okay if Eshana came home with me? You can call us if you need her. My dad will bring her right away."

"Of course," said Eshana's mom. "The doctors say Suneesh is stable for now.

There's no point in us all waiting here. I have Dina with me. You're a good friend to my Eshana. Thank you, Pia." She kissed Pia's forehead.

Eshana felt even worse. She had still not said another word to her mother. Dina Aunty was glaring at her. Eshana hugged her mom tight. She hoped her mom would understand how sorry she was. How much Eshana loved her. Her mother gave her a weak smile and sat down again.

Eshana left the hospital with Pia. Only when they were outside did she speak. "Ignore any mean stuff I say. I can't help it," she confessed. "And what's the deal with those shoes? They're so ugly!"

Pia looked down at her shoes and then back up at her friend. She looked very confused.

Eshana told Pia the whole story.

"And if I don't fix this, Dad's going to die," said Eshana. Then she burst into tears.

Chapter Nine

Pia thought for a moment. "I have an idea. You should try to do some good stuff. If you can manage to keep that big mouth shut."

Eshana stared at her. "Awesome. Why didn't I think of that, you troll?"

"We both know I'm the one with the brains!" said Pia, smiling. "Just do as I say."

Eshana hugged Pia. "Let's go to your place. It's basic, but it'll do."

As they waited for the bus, a scruffy-looking man stopped and asked them for money. Eshana almost told him to piss off. But she caught Pia's eye and remembered the plan. She pulled some cookies out of her backpack. She handed them to the man, along with some change she'd found at the bottom of the backpack.

"Thank you," said the man. "God bless you."

Eshana smiled. She was doing it. She was fighting Wise One!

On the bus, an old woman almost toppled onto her lap. After giving her a rude look, Eshana offered the old woman her seat.

"Thank you, my dear," she said. "It's lovely to meet a young person with such good manners."

Maybe if she did enough good deeds, she could beat the evil Wise One and save her dad. But first she had to try and undo what she had done. She texted Gina and told her she wasn't coming on the ski trip.

At Pia's house, Eshana went online and directly to the chat room. Wise One was waiting for her.

You're going to be rich, Raven! You must be so happy.

Pia talked Eshana out of typing what she really wanted to say. The idea was to undo the damage, not make him mad.

I take back my wish, Wise One. I don't want to be rich.

I'm afraid that is impossible. Once you write it down, it's set in motion. That's the way it works.

That meant her dad would die so they would get the insurance money. Eshana wanted to throw up again. Her hands shook so much she could barely type.

Please. I'll do anything. Just stop this wish and let my dad live.

Anything?

Anything, Wise One.

Type it out.

"Bad idea," whispered Pia.

Eshana shrugged and typed, **I will do anything you ask.**

Excellent. Log on tomorrow for further instructions.

Eshana wandered the website. A few others tried chatting with her, but she ignored them and logged off. As soon as she and Pia had finished dinner, Eshana called her mom.

Her mother sounded relieved, almost happy. "Suneesh is doing much better," she said. "He even managed to eat some soup. The doctor says that's an excellent sign. If he continues like this, he may come home next week."

"That's great, Mom," said Eshana. Luckily, nothing mean slipped out.

Eshana went for a quick walk to clear her head. She was glad Pia had decided to stay behind and do some homework. It was hard work not saying terrible things!

She thought about everything that had happened. The site and Wise One were dangerous. She knew that now. Asking for a wish wasn't simple. There was always a price. Someone got hurt. Maybe even someone you loved. T&T had warned her to be careful. If only she'd listened.

But didn't everyone have dreams and desires? Who wouldn't say yes to someone who promised to make them come true? There was a weight on Eshana's chest making it difficult to breathe. It was almost as if Wise One could hear her thoughts and was punishing her. Eshana had to figure out a way to stop him before more people got hurt.

"I have to shut this site down," said Eshana to Pia as soon as she got back. "I have an idea. One of the problems Ms. Buckley gave us to solve today made me think of it. Maybe we could introduce a computer virus somehow. But I don't know if I can do it on my own. I'll need help."

They both looked at each other. "Tito," they said in unison.

"Tito has been really worried about you," Pia added. "They told me to call you when you didn't come back from the principal's office."

Tito had always been a good friend. Even if Eshana hadn't realized it. Ryan only wanted to copy her work. What a fool she'd been.

Pia and Tito were better friends than Ryan and all those other people.

Pia texted Tito, and within minutes they were on group chat.

Girl, basic rule online is to not get into weird sites! You know that.

Cut the lecture, Tito. What's the plan?

Pia always got straight to the point. Eshana loved that. She jumped in.

We have to shut this site down. Met one person on there who warned me. But hey, wishes!!!

At a price. No freebies.

So you'll help? Eshana couldn't help thinking of her dad in the hospital. What if he didn't make it?

I got your back! 😊

Pia dropped her phone and high-fived Eshana.

Eshana knew she could beat Wise One. With her *real* friends.

Chapter Ten

They worked late into the night. Tito seemed to know *exactly* what to do. Almost as if they'd been to the site before. Around midnight they texted Eshana and Pia.

Good to go!

Thanks, Tito, Eshana replied.

Ditto, Pia texted.

Just don't visit any weird sites again. K?

Eshana and Pia both texted back, **KK!**

School was a drag the next day. But somehow Eshana got through it with Pia's and Tito's help. She spoke as little as possible, just in case. Her thoughts were with her dad. Her mother had called to say he was doing better, but Eshana was still worried.

Eshana stayed at Pia's again. After dinner they headed to Pia's room. Tito had set up a secure group chat where they could also share screens. It was time to do this.

Eshana wiped her sweaty palms on her jeans and logged on. Within seconds Wise One greeted her.

Hello, Raven! How is your father?

He's fine. What do you want?

Come now. I work so hard to make you and the others happy, and now you're upset. Do you want another wish? Is that it?

No thanks. I won't be back, Wise One.

Not so fast, Raven. You promised to do something for me.

Fine. What?

Tito sent a note to the group chat.

Slow down and be polite. Wise One is dangerous. Don't make him mad.

OK

Pia made a rude gesture at the wizard avatar.

"Cut that out," whispered Eshana. "I need to focus."

Eshana noticed that there were very few people on the site now.

Where's everyone, Wise One?

Once they get their wishes, they leave. People today are so selfish. Now you're going to leave too, but not before you introduce me to a friend.

Don't have any. Or I wouldn't be here.

Lies! I need the truth, remember? You must have at least one friend. If not for me, do this for your father. You don't want to lose him, do you?

Eshana felt sick. She took a deep breath.

Pia shook her head. "What a jerk!" she whispered.

Tito told Eshana to keep Wise One chatting. They needed time to set it all up. Eshana still wasn't sure what *it* was. But she knew this was probably her only chance to shut the site down. No way was she getting another victim for Wise One. She knew it meant her dad might still be in danger. But she had to keep calm and play along. She replied to Wise One.

There is someone who might like this site. I gave her the details. But I don't see her online yet.

Call her and tell her to get on, Raven. This site works best when I have lots of people making wishes.

Give me a minute.

I won't wait forever. And you'd better not try to be clever. I've been around a lot longer than you think, kiddo. 😉

Eshana's skin prickled. How had she not realized how dangerous Wise One was? She sent a message to Tito.

Are you done yet? This weirdo is getting desperate. I don't think I can stall any longer.

His website firewalls are solid, girl. I need a few more minutes to tunnel through.

Wise One was getting impatient.

If you're planning on backing down on your promise, I suggest you think twice. Remember your dad.

Pia and Eshana stared at each other. Any minute now she could get a call saying that her dad had died. Eshana had to do something. Fast!

"Give me your laptop and take mine," she said to Pia.

Pia handed it over. Eshana went to the *I-WISH* site and logged on. She created a user name—Pi.

"What are you doing?" Pia asked.

"Trust me!" said Eshana. "Pretend to be Raven and keep chatting with Wise One. Describe the day. Put up some crying emojis. We have to give Tito enough time to set this up."

As soon as Pia logged on, Eshana took her own computer back. She was Raven again, and Pia was Pi.

Give it a break, Wise One. Here's my friend, Pi. I told you I would keep my promise.

Hello, Pi, and welcome to this site. I am your guide, Wise One.

Cool site, W.O. Raven's raved about this

place. So how many wishes do I get?

I like a girl who gets right to the point. How many do you want?

A gazillion?

Funny. Why don't we start with one, Pi.

Eshana remembered what Wise One had told her. When she wanted to take back her last wish. It was set in motion as soon as it was written down. It was worth a try.

I want this site to disappear.

Wise One's avatar, which had somehow turned angry, filled the screen. There were some cracks and hisses, and then both laptops shut down.

Eshana stared at Pia. "You think we did it? Did we shut him down by using his wishes against him?"

"Nah, it couldn't be that easy," said Pia. "Where the hell is Tito? Why aren't they helping?"

Their computers started to reboot. Eshana watched the screens come to life, her heart pounding. The group chat with Tito showed up.

Not bad, right? 😊

Pia dialed Tito's number and put them on speakerphone.

"What do you mean, 'not bad'?" said Pia. "*We* were the ones who wished this guy out of existence!"

"Nope," Tito replied. "I got my virus—I call it MURK—in there and destroyed the bastard. You're welcome!"

"Give me a minute before I bow to you,

Lord Tito," said Eshana. "I need to call Mom."

Her mother picked up on the first ring. Her dad was doing very well, she told Eshana. He would definitely be home by next week.

"Looks like all is well," said Eshana when she'd ended the call. "Thanks so much to you both. I couldn't have done this without you."

"You're treating us to coffee at that French bakery," said Pia. "It's a little pricey, but we're worth it, right, Tito?"

"What about high tea at the Tea and Tattle?" said Tito. "Not a coffee fan. Tea and toast are my faves."

That's when Eshana realized something. "You! It was *you* on I-WISH!" she said.

"Guilty as charged," said Tito. "Tried to get you out of there too. Dropped hints the size of bloody elephants. But yeah, I did some digging and realized this site was bad news. I'm glad that we managed to shut it down. Could have been the wish that did it. But I think it was my superior programming skills."

Eshana laughed, feeling light as a feather now. "Maybe you're right. High tea it is. And then I think we should go visit Cara and take her some flowers. You never know what someone might be wishing for."

Acknowledgments

Thanks to my awesome editor, Tanya, who helps me see the forest *and* the trees. Thanks to the entire Orca pod for continuing to believe in me. Love to my family and friends for always being super supportive. Finally, thanks to my agent, Naomi, who is my rock.

Has Jaylin received
a message from
beyond the grave?

Chapter One

Jamal tries to hand the bottle of beer to me. "Come on, Jaylin," he says. "Just one drink."

I shake my head. "You know I don't drink. Besides, I can't stay. I have to study." I look down at my watch. "It's already eight thirty-five. I should've been home by now."

I look around the room. There are about twenty people from our school here. Even though we're in the middle of exams, the music is loud, and most people are up and dancing. The party is just getting started. No one seems too worried about studying. No one, that is, but me. Truth is, for most of the people here, exams won't be a huge problem. But what Jamal doesn't know is that for me, an English exam is like climbing Mount Everest. There's a reason I need a lot of time to study. And that reason is the only secret I've ever kept from Jamal.

Jamal rolls his eyes at me. "You're the smartest girl I know. You've been studying for this English exam forever. And it's not even for another two days. Don't you want to hang with me?" Jamal gives me the sad puppy-dog-eyes look.

"Honestly. I just…can't," I say. My mouth feels like I've eaten a big spoonful of peanut butter. I stand up and grab my bag. "I'm sorry. Call you later?"

Jamal shrugs. "Sure. If you can fit me in." He looks around the room. I know he's upset. We haven't spent much time together in the last few weeks. It's just a really hard time for me right now, and he doesn't get it.

I lean over and give him a fast kiss. "I'll call you," I say. I head across the room toward the front door. As I'm about to leave, I look back to wave goodbye to Jamal.

He's sitting beside Vicky Mars on the couch. Their heads are bent close together.

And they're laughing at something on her phone. Vicky puts her hand on Jamal's upper leg. My cheeks start to burn.

I've got to get out of here. Now.

I pull open the front door and race out to the sidewalk. Tears spilling down my cheeks, I run all the way home.

"Jaylin? Is that you?" Mom calls from the kitchen. "What have I told you about slamming that door?"

"Yeah. It's me," I say. I kick off my shoes and wipe at my eyes. I don't want Mom to see me upset. She already doesn't have much love for Jamal.

Mom wheels into the front hall. She looks up at me from her chair and smiles.

"Why are you standing out here? I've made your favorite. Pizza, with lots of extra cheese. Just the way you like it."

"I'm sorry, Mom," I say. I lean down and give her a kiss on the cheek. Her skin smells like warm vanilla. For some reason that makes me want to start to cry again. "I ate at the library with Alex. I'm super sorry."

Mom's brown eyes darken with worry. She knows I'm not telling the truth. I have not hung out with any of my friends for almost a year.

"Well, make sure you take a break at some point. I know this time of year is hard." She shoots me a sad smile as she turns her wheelchair around to go back to the kitchen. "And if you want to watch some Netflix with me tonight, I'd like that." She pauses. "I miss her too, you know."

"Maybe, if I get enough done," I say.

I go upstairs, lie down on my bed and open my computer. I still have to study. Our class has been reading *Dracula*—a novel I understand on a deep level. People think it's just about vampires. But the main theme is wanting the people you love to live forever. I get that. When you lose someone you really love, like I have, you'd do anything to keep them with you.

Time to hit the books. I've been given a version of *Dracula* that my computer can read out loud. Because I have dyslexia, when I'm reading my brain doesn't work the same as the brain of someone without dyslexia does. But it doesn't mean I'm not smart. I have the second-highest mark in my class. And I worked my butt off to get that grade.

After an hour of studying, it's time for a brain break. I check my Instagram first. There's a message. I need to see who has been sending me some Instagram love. It had better be Jamal. He's got some explaining to do.

I click on the message.

Hey, girl! I love you and I miss you. I know it must be a shock to read this. But it's me. For real. And I need your help. I need you to go to our spot tomorrow.

x Fatima

This must be a sick joke. Someone has hacked my best friend's account.

I slam my computer shut. My hands are shaking so hard, I have to sit on them just to think. Maybe I'm dreaming. Yeah, that must be it. I'll go to bed and everything will be okay when I wake up.

After all, there's no way this can be real. Because Fatima died exactly one year ago today.

Mahtab Narsimhan is the award-winning author of several books for young readers, including *Embrace the Chicken*, *Mission Mumbai*, *The Tiffin* and *The Third Eye*, which won the Silver Birch Award. She was a Writer in Residence at the Toronto District School Board from 2014 to 2016. Born in Mumbai, Mahtab immigrated to Canada in 1997. She now lives in Vancouver, British Columbia.

For more information on all the books

in the Orca Anchor line, please visit

orcabook.com